ONE POTATO, TWO POTATO

Cynthia DeFelice

Pictures by Andrea U'Ren

Farrar, Straus and Giroux • New York

In memory of Michael Smith,
merry Irish elf,
and Caroline and Ellison Woodworth,
the original Mr. and Mrs. O'Grady
—C.D.

For Grandmother, Alice Douglas Burns,
and for Grandpa, Harold U'Ren
—A.U.

Text copyright © 2006 by Cynthia C. DeFelice
Illustrations copyright © 2006 by Andrea U'Ren
All rights reserved
Distributed in Canada by Douglas & McIntyre Ltd.
Color separations by Chroma Graphics PTE Ltd.
Printed and bound in the United States of America by Phoenix Color Corporation
Designed by Nancy Goldenberg
First edition, 2006
10 9 8 7 6 5 4 3 2

www.fsgkidsbooks.com

Library of Congress Cataloging-in-Publication Data
DeFelice, Cynthia C.
    One potato, two potato / Cynthia DeFelice ; pictures by Andrea U'Ren.— 1st ed.
       p.   cm.
    Summary: A very poor, humble couple live so simple a life they share everything, until
the husband discovers a pot with magical powers buried under the very last potato in the garden.
    ISBN-13: 978-0-374-35640-8
    ISBN-10: 0-374-35640-8
    [1. Fairy tales.   2. Potatoes—Fiction.]   I. U'Ren, Andrea, ill.   II. Title.

PZ8.D35On 2006
[E]—dc22
                                                            2004047217

Mr. and Mrs. O'Grady lived alone on a bare and rocky hillside. Their children had grown up long ago and gone out into the great wide world to seek their fortunes. But Mr. and Mrs. O'Grady stayed behind in their cottage, where they had little and shared everything.

Mr. and Mrs. O'Grady were so poor they dug one potato from their little garden every day, called it breakfast, lunch, and supper, and considered themselves lucky to have it.

They were so skinny they could sit side by side on one chair to eat their meal,
and it was a good thing, too, because one chair was all they had.

Mrs. O'Grady had only one hairpin. Together, they had but one blanket full
of holes, and one raggedy coat, which they took turns wearing in the winter.

They had just one candle, which they never burned. Every evening, as the sun went down and darkness was nigh, Mrs. O'Grady pretended to light the candle. And every morning, when the sun rose and light filled their little house, she pretended to blow out the candle.

They had one gold coin, which they were saving for a rainy day, and which they kept tucked under the straw of their mattress.

Now, Mr. O'Grady was as fine a husband as Mrs. O'Grady could have wanted. Yet it was the wish of her heart to have a friend, someone with whom she could share recipes for boiled potatoes and sweet memories of how it felt to touch her newborn babies' downy heads.

To be sure, Mrs. O'Grady was the finest wife Mr. O'Grady could imagine. Yet he, too, longed for a friend, someone with whom he could discuss potato weevils and root rot.

One day, Mr. O'Grady was out digging in the potato patch for their meal, as he did every day. To his dismay, he saw that he had come to the very last potato in the very last row of the garden. Hoping he had somehow missed one, he dug a wee bit deeper.

What was this? It was harder than a potato, bigger than a potato, blacker than a potato . . . Why, it was a *pot*! Mr. O'Grady was quite surprised that he had never come across it before in that tiny garden, and he wanted to show the curious object to his wife. Since he needed both hands to carry it, he put the last potato into the pot and started for home.

"Mrs. O'Grady, come quickly!" he called.

Mrs. O'Grady rushed to the door. "What have you got there, husband?"

"Well," said Mr. O'Grady, setting the pot on the floor, "it's a pot."

"Aye, so it is," said Mrs. O'Grady. "But it's much too big for cooking."

"So far, it's come in handy for carrying our last potato home."

"Our last potato!" exclaimed Mrs. O'Grady. "Saints have mercy! Whatever will we do?" She leaned over the pot to reach for the potato. As she did, her hairpin fell out of her hair and into the pot. She paid it little mind, though, for inside the pot were *two* potatoes. She held them up. "Husband," she scolded, "you oughtn't joke about such things!"

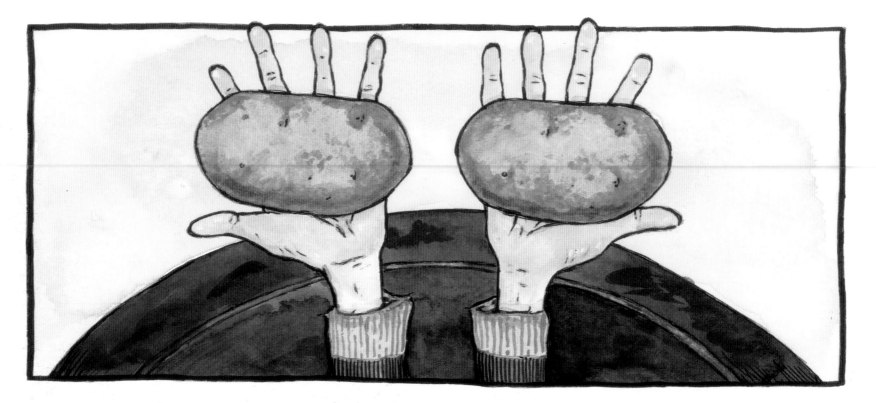

"But I wasn't joking," said Mr. O'Grady, befuddled by the sight of the second potato. "I put only one potato into the pot."

Mrs. O'Grady smiled. "And only one hairpin fell into the pot. I suppose that now I will find two?" She reached into the pot and her face grew pale. When she withdrew her hands, they held not one but two hairpins, exactly alike. "Husband, how can this be?" she whispered.

Mr. O'Grady took one of the hairpins and threw it into the pot. Quickly, he reached back in and pulled out two hairpins.

"Now I have three hairpins instead of one!" Mrs. O'Grady said. Happily, she began arranging her hair.

Mr. O'Grady said, "Wife, think! Surely this pot is magic! If it made another potato and two more hairpins, what do you think would happen if we put in"—he looked around the room—"our candle?"

Mrs. O'Grady ran to get the candle and tossed it into the pot. Sure enough, she pulled out two candles so exactly alike that one couldn't tell the old one from the new.

Next, Mr. O'Grady put their coat into the pot. Out came another coat, as raggedy and torn as the first!

Then in went the blanket, and out came two blankets, with holes in the exact same places.

Mrs. O'Grady hugged her husband. "We will both be warm this winter!" she said.

Mr. O'Grady took the two potatoes, placed them in the pot, and pulled out four. He threw the four potatoes into the pot and took out eight. And when he put in the eight potatoes, sixteen potatoes were waiting to be pulled from the pot! Soon the O'Gradys had enough potatoes for a feast.

Mrs. O'Grady made herself a whole set of new hairpins and enough candles to light their nights through the darkest winter.

Mr. O'Grady tried to put the chair into the pot, but it didn't quite fit. "No matter," he said. "One chair has served us well for a long time."

But Mrs. O'Grady, who was a clever woman, had been thinking. She went over to the mattress and, with trembling fingers, took out the gold coin. "Husband," she said, "do you suppose the pot's magic will work on this?"

Holding her breath, she tossed the coin into the pot. That one coin became two! Then two became four, four became eight, eight became sixteen, and soon the floor was covered with bright gold coins.

Mr. O'Grady put several of the coins into his pocket. "Dear wife, I am going to the village to buy you a new coat, a new blanket, and a new chair."

Mrs. O'Grady waved goodbye to her husband. She put the potatoes into a sack. She gathered up the coins and placed them under the mattress. Then she went outside, where she found a single flower growing on the bare and rocky hillside. Soon she had a bouquet of flowers just like it.

Tired out from all the excitement, Mrs. O'Grady wrapped herself in both blankets and took a nap. She was awakened by her husband's cheerful whistle as he came through the door, his arms filled with packages.

Eager to see what he had brought, Mrs. O'Grady ran to meet him. She tripped and fell . . .

and landed headfirst, right in the pot! "Help me out of here, husband!" she cried.

Packages flew through the air as Mr. O'Grady raced over to the pot. There
were his wife's skinny little legs, sticking out of the top, kicking back and forth.

Mr. O'Grady grabbed on tightly, pulled poor old Mrs. O'Grady out of the pot, and set her gently on the floor.

But, saints have mercy! Now there were two more skinny little legs, kicking back and forth. Without thinking, Mr. O'Grady reached into the pot, grabbed those skinny little legs, and pulled out . . . *another* Mrs. O'Grady, so exactly like his wife that he could scarcely tell the difference.

"Oh dear, oh woe," Mr. O'Grady moaned. "One wife is all I ever wanted."

When the first Mrs. O'Grady had recovered from her surprise, she smiled and said, "There's only one thing to be done."

Mr. O'Grady pointed to the second Mrs. O'Grady. "Throw her back in?"

"Not at all," said the first Mrs. O'Grady. "You, husband, must jump into the pot yourself."

"Jump into the pot! But then there will be two of me, as well."

"Quite so," said the first Mrs. O'Grady. "Then we will have a wife for each husband, and a husband for each wife. And best of all," she added happily, "you will have a friend at last, and so will I."

Mr. O'Grady thought for a moment. He took a deep breath and jumped headfirst into the pot. His worn leather boots stuck out of the top.

Together, the two Mrs. O'Gradys grabbed on to the boots and pulled out Mr. O'Grady.

Sure enough, now there were two more boots
sticking out of the top. Both Mrs. O'Gradys
grabbed on to those boots and pulled out . . .
another Mr. O'Grady, so like the first that they
could scarcely tell the difference.

The O'Gradys—all four of them—looked at one another. As they talked, they realized they had a great deal in common. Already they felt like the closest of friends. The first Mr. and Mrs. O'Grady agreed that the new Mr. and Mrs. O'Grady made a handsome couple indeed.

Over a candlelight supper of two potatoes each, the Mrs. O'Gradys spoke happily of babies and booties, while the Mr. O'Gradys discussed potato weevils and root rot. Afterward, the first Mrs. O'Grady wrapped her arms around the pot and said, "Thank you." Then she said to the others, "Surely we have everything we could possibly want. Let us bury this wonderful pot for someone else to find."

So they did. And from that day forward, all of the O'Gradys lived happily together. They were, they liked to say, simply *beside themselves* with joy.